The Monster Storm

A Red Fox Book
Published by Random House Children's Books
20 Vauxhall Bridge Road, London SW1V 2SA
A division of The Random House Group Ltd
London Melbourne Sydney Auckland
Johannesburg and agencies throughout the world

Text copyright © Jeanne Willis 1995
Illustrations copyright © Susan Varley 1995

3 5 7 9 10 8 6 4 2

First published in Great Britain by Andersen Press Ltd 1995
Red Fox edition 1997
This edition 2000

Printed in Singapore by Tien Wah Press (PTE) Ltd

THE RANDOM HOUSE GROUP Ltd Reg. No. 954009
www.randomhouse.co.uk

The Monster Storm

WRITTEN BY JEANNE WILLIS
ILLUSTRATED BY SUSAN VARLEY

RED
FOX

Dennis the monster was five and a bit
And not very scary, I have to admit.
He was kind to dumb animals, insects and plants
And gave up his seat to his elderly aunts.

He did as his mother said, and, without fail,
Never crossed roads without holding her tail.

He shared all his sweets and his favourite toys
With his small sister Dorothy, unlike most boys.

The fairies made fun of him he was so tame,
Except, I'm afraid, when a thunderstorm came.

It happened on Tuesday. A terrible storm
Came out of the blue. It was windless and warm
And Dennis was riding about in the back
When he heard a huge bang and a terrible crack.

He fell off his bike and he shouted out loud,
"Help, I am being attacked by a cloud!"

He picked himself up and broke into a run.
"It's after me, Mummy! It's firing a gun!"

"Nonsense," his mother said, "don't be afraid.
It's only the angels' brass band being played.

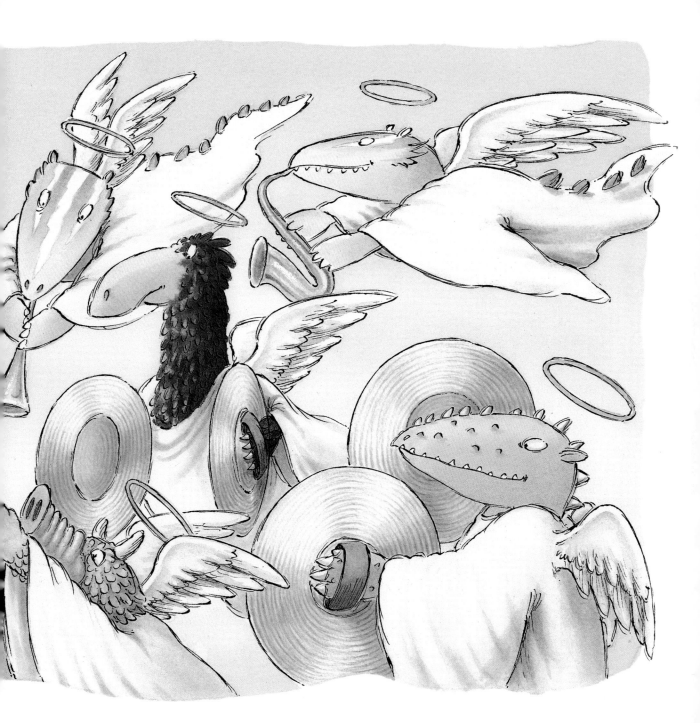

They're having a concert up there in the sky."
But Dennis suspected that this was a lie.

He gathered a kettle, some pots and some pans,
Some spoons and some sticks and some empty tin cans,

Some bricks, some balloons and a hammer and nails,
His mother's best china and several pails.

"Where are you off to Dennis? Come here,"
His mother said, " take an umbrella, my dear!
It's pouring with rain, you'll be soaked to the skin."
But Dennis ran off. "I am not coming in!
I am going to frighten that storm cloud away!"
Roared Dennis, quite rudely, I'm sorry to say.

He raced through the wood, took a left at the Mill,

Then climbed to the top of Old Rabbit Hole Hill.

He put the tin saucepan on just like a hat
And hit it with cutlery, loudly. "Take that!"
He yelled at the cloud and he battered and crashed
With the pots and the plates until all of them smashed.

The cloud drifted off and the moon shimmered white
But Dennis kept clashing and bashing all night.
He saw and heard nothing, for to his surprise
The saucepan had jammed past his ears and eyes.
He pulled and he tugged but without any luck -
He'd hit it so hard that the saucepan had stuck,

And as he attempted to rescue his head
He made enough noise to awaken the dead.

Deep in a burrow, a small rabbit cried.
He called for his mother, who hopped to his side.
She saw he was frightened and, mopping his tears,
She spoke to him tenderly, stroking his ears,
"It's only a thunderstorm. Sleep if you can,
It isn't a monster attacking a pan.

Monsters aren't real, they are make-believe things
Like pixies and goblins and horses with wings,

Imaginary creatures that live in a book.
You still don't believe me? Then let's go and look..."

Some bestselling Red Fox picture books